Never forget whose you are.

To:_______________________________

From:_____________________________

Date:_____________________________

May you always hear the Shepherd's voice
in the stillness of the morning.

Colocho:

A Sheep on the Beach

Curtis Koch

First Edition: 2025

Published by Worship at Sunrise LLC
www.worshipatsunrise.com

CONTENTS

INVITATION TO READER

This book is a fable—a journey of surrender, stillness, and awakening.

It is meant to be felt as much as understood.

You'll find poetry and prayer, journal entries and whispers—

woven like tide and time.

Not every thread is tied.

Some truths are not explained, but carried.

So let the story move like waves—

quiet, steady, and alive.

And listen.

Not just to the words,

but to the voice behind them.

The Shepherd still speaks.

Sometimes through waves.

Sometimes through sheep.

And sometimes… through you.

PROLOGUE:

The Night That Stirred the Sea

Before Surrender...Before Dawn

THE MOON WAS FULL THE night Colocho first saw the ocean. It rose like a quiet lantern in the sky, casting silver across the waves until the water looked like glass—fragile, deep, and waiting. The air paused, as if the stars were listening, not shining.

He wasn't supposed to be out this far. But something had drawn him past the fence, past the dunes, past the worn paths of the pasture. His hooves sank into the cool sand—unsure, but unafraid. The sea stretched out before him, vast and unknowable.

On a nearby dune, half-shadowed by a crooked fence, a young man stood barefoot in the grass.

There was nothing spectacular about the moment—

No lightning, no storm.

Just moonlight and stillness.

But something about the scene unsettled him.

They just stood, two watchers on opposite ends of the night, held in the presence of something greater than either could explain.

But that night…

…was still weeks away.

CHAPTER 1:

Before the Beach

Before the Waves... Before the Call

THE CLATTER OF SILVERWARE AND sizzle of oil had once been his music. The young man had spent most of his twenties in the back rooms of restaurants—flipping, plating, fixing, shouting, and pacing.

He wasn't just a cook. He was the kitchen guy. Reliable. Efficient. Fast. If it needed doing, he got it done. If someone fell short, he filled the gap.

For a long time, that was enough. The kitchen was chaos he could control. And that control made him feel safe.

He lived in an apartment over a laundromat on the east side of town. The air always smelled like detergent and old grease.

His walls were bare except for two things: a faded photo of his grandmother—Bible in one hand and pie in the other—and a handwritten recipe from her, tucked beneath a chipped magnet on the fridge.

He had a truck he loved—old, beat-up, but dependable. It had taken him to every job he'd ever had. Every late-night grocery run. Every 3 a.m. shift. The occasional fishing trip to the surf.

Until one night, it didn't.

It was late. Rain.

Headlights in the wrong lane.

A horn that didn't come soon enough.

The truck spun.

So did his life.

He limped away with bruised ribs and a broken leg. But the job? Gone. No room for crutches in the kitchen.

The apartment? Month-to-month. And he was already two weeks behind. Friends? They drifted.

You learn quickly who's around when the adrenaline stops.

He had nothing but a trash bag of clothes, a tent from college, a journal, and an old leather Bible his grandmother had left behind. He hadn't opened it in years. Not since the funeral. Not since the last time he prayed—if you could even call it that.

Bargaining with a God who never responded.

So he drove to the coast in a borrowed car, looking for somewhere quiet. Somewhere cheap. Somewhere no one would ask about the bruises on his spirit or the weight in his eyes.

That's how he found the trailer.

It was sun-bleached, dented, and smelled faintly of mildew and salt. But it was his—for now.

He parked it at the edge of a forgotten pasture just off the dunes, tucked between a row of old palms and the broken fence line of someone else's land.

And for a while, he did nothing.

Didn't walk the beach.

Didn't cook.

Didn't speak to anyone—unless it was the cashier at the gas station or the fisherman two lots down who nodded more than he talked.

He slept too long.

Ate too little.

Scrolled endlessly through old texts he never sent and pictures he couldn't delete.

The silence, at first, felt like punishment. Later, it started to feel like mourning.

He thought about the fiancée he almost married.

The friend he cut off during a fight that still replayed in his head.

The temper he couldn't always control.

The family he barely called—even when things were good. Especially when they were good.

He didn't know how to say *I'm sorry* anymore. Didn't know if it would matter if he did.

One night, curled in the corner of the trailer while a storm lashed the windows, he found his grandmother's Bible again.

He opened it—not to read, but to see if her handwriting still lived in the margins.

It did.

The Lord is my shepherd; I shall not want.

The young man stared at those words until the pages blurred.

In the weeks that followed, something inside him began to ache. Not the kind of ache that wants escape, but the kind that longs to be found.

He didn't know what he was waiting for—only that the life he had known was no longer something he could return to.

He needed peace. But more than that, he needed permission to start again.

CHAPTER 2:

The Gentle Current

Surrender...In the Flow of the Tide

THE MOON WAS FULL THE night Colocho first heard the call. It hung low and bright over the shoreline, casting silver light across the sand like a path meant just for him.

He had never ventured this close to the water before, but something within him stirred—something older than fear, deeper than instinct.

The ocean whispered in waves that made his hooves tremble.

Colocho was not like the other sheep. His wool curled in soft waves, and unlike the flocks that grazed inland, his face, legs, and belly were bare—open to the elements, exposed yet unharmed.

The others called him peculiar, but Colocho had begun to see his differences not as burdens, but as quiet blessings.

That morning, as dawn stretched its golden fingers across the sky, Colocho waited at the edge of the ocean, hooves sinking into damp sand. The waves lapped gently—inviting, but unknown. He took a step closer.

Then—a voice.

Not like the human voices singing nearby, but deeper. More ancient.

It echoed not through his ears, but through his chest.

Colocho turned instinctively, but all he saw was water and light.

A crab appeared beside him—one claw larger than the other, shell glinting like polished stone. It drifted with the retreating tide, calm and unhurried.

"Doesn't that scare you?" Colocho called out. "Not knowing where you'll end up?"

The crab clicked softly. "More scary to fight it. Current's going to win anyway." His voice was scratchy but kind. "You know how to surrender?"

"Surrender?" Colocho repeated. The word felt foreign—yet needed.

"Letting go. Trusting the flow instead of fighting it. Water knows where it's going. Question is—do you trust it enough to find out?"

Colocho stepped deeper. The water kissed his ankles, then his knees. Then came a larger wave.

He panicked—legs scrambling, hooves slipping, water in his nose.

The crab called out, "Trust God, and He will protect you!"

"Who is God?" Colocho sputtered.

"The sheep call Him the Shepherd. Surrender to Him. Pray!"

Colocho stopped flailing. And for the first time in his life, he prayed.

He let go.

The wave, instead of drowning him, cradled him—lifting and returning him gently to the shore.

When he opened his eyes, he lay on the sand, soaked but breathing. Lighter. Not just in body—but in soul.

The crab appeared beside him. "Not bad for your first try."

"I thought I would drown."

"You didn't. You floated. You trusted. Most don't."

They sat in silence for a while. The crab shifted in his shell.

"I used to be afraid too," the crab said. "But every time I grow, I leave my shell behind. I trust the Shepherd to give me another."

Colocho turned his face to the rising sun. "Will He forgive me? For all I've done?"

"All you have to do is faithfully ask Him. That's surrender too. He knows we'll fall. But He loves us anyway."

That morning, Colocho learned the first truth of the journey: surrender was not weakness—it was trust.

I thought I was sinking.

But when I let go…

I floated.

I didn't know trust could carry me like that.

Colocho…that afternoon…returns to the pasture…

That afternoon, Colocho returned to the pasture. Salt clung to his legs, but his eyes were steady.

The other sheep lifted their heads. The older sheep approached.

"You went to the shoreline again," she said. "What did you find?"

Colocho hesitated. "I was afraid. I almost drowned."

Murmurs rippled through the flock.

"But I didn't," he added. "I let go. I prayed. And the Shepherd carried me back."

The lambs moved closer.

The old sheep tilted her head. "You believe He heard you?"

Colocho nodded. "I didn't hear Him in words, but I felt Him in the water. In the safety. In the peace afterward."

One lamb whispered, "Were you changed?"

"Yes," Colocho said quietly. "I'm not the same. I trust Him now. Or at least—I want to."

And for the first time, the others listened— not with suspicion, but with curiosity.

A few followed him toward the hilltop. He wasn't sure if he was leading— but he wasn't alone.

The Young Man's Night

Earlier that day, the young man had finally unpacked what little he had. Inside the trailer, he hung up two things on the peeling wood-paneled wall: a faded photo of his grandmother—Bible in one hand, pie in the other— and a handwritten recipe she'd given him years ago, curled at the edges and stained with flour.

He didn't know why he brought them. Maybe they were the only things that still made him feel…known.

He'd cleared the lot that morning—raked away the driftwood and catchweed creeping in from the dunes, stacking the brittle wood in a corner. The grass was patchy, stubborn. Half sand. Half soil.

But he swept a path with his boots, dragged old bricks into a circle, and found a few broken stones buried in the grass and added them too.

It wasn't much. But it was something.

A fire pit now sat in the center of the lot. A place to sit. Or think. Or maybe just…burn things.

He'd even found an old rusty grill behind the trailer, half covered in seaweed and mouse droppings. He scrubbed it out with steel wool and dish soap, letting it dry in the sun.

There was no propane. But one day, maybe.

Maybe he'd cook again. Maybe.

That evening, in the fading glow of the pasture, he leaned on the fence. Colocho grazed nearby.

He still didn't understand the strange sheep. But something about him— something in the quiet way he moved— felt like a question the young man hadn't asked yet.

When he reached out to touch Colocho's curls, something small tumbled free: a polished hermit crab shell.

He lifted it to his ear.

Yahweh.

It wasn't sound, not exactly. But it stirred something deep.

Later that night, he sat at the window, the shell cupped in his palm. The word echoed in his mind like breath.

Yahweh.

The silence in the trailer didn't feel so heavy now. Just…waiting.

He opened the leather-bound journal and wrote for the first time.

Morning Coffee: A Promise

The next morning, he woke early—not from anxiety or noise, but from a quiet urge.

He stepped outside barefoot, mug in hand, and let the steam rise.

The pasture was bathed in fog. The world hadn't spoken yet. And he liked it that way.

He thought of the shell. Of surrender. Of the strange sheep who carried it in his wool. Of his own grip on things he couldn't control.

Maybe surrender wasn't the end. Maybe it was the beginning.

He sipped the coffee slowly.

For once, he didn't rush.

This—this stillness—was enough.

And so, with the sun still rising, he made a promise:

Tomorrow, he would wake again. Coffee in hand. And he would remember what the day before had taught him.

Journal Entry—Colocho's Talking Shell

Met a sheep on the beach today. Don't know if he has a name. I started calling him Colocho—Curly one, in Spanish. It fits.

A hermit crab shell fell out of his wool. I picked it up.

It made a sound but almost a word... "Ya wey?"

Not sure if I imagined it. But it sounded important. Sacred, almost.

I felt like giving up this week. Felt like I quit.

But maybe... maybe surrender isn't quitting. Maybe it's giving in.

Giving in to something better.

CHAPTER 3:

The Stillness of Morning

Unhurried Time...In the First Light

THE FOLLOWING MONTH, COLOCHO RETURNED to the beach before the first light touched the sky. The memory of the waves' embrace lingered—soft, rhythmic, unshakeable.

This time, he didn't step into the water. Instead, he lay on the cool sand and waited.

There was a quiet that came before the dawn. It wasn't silence exactly—there was the rhythmic hush of waves, the distant cries of gulls—but it felt peaceful. Unrushed. Whole.

Colocho curled his legs beneath him, breathing in the salt air. He noticed how the world moved slowly here. No one was in a hurry. Even the waves resisted hurry; they reached the shore in their own time.

And still, they were always on time.

A soft scraping sound came from his left. Colocho turned and saw a young sea turtle, slowly crawling toward the water.

She moved with effort, but not panic. It seemed deliberate. Chosen.

"You're up early too," Colocho said.

The turtle paused and looked at him. "The morning is the only time the beach belongs to itself."

Colocho tilted his head. "Why do you come back, even when it's hard?"

The turtle settled into a sandy dip. "Because the stillness teaches me who I am. The world is loud, but the morning whispers."

They sat in silence for a while. The turtle's eyes closed, but she was not asleep—only resting, breathing.

Colocho lowered his voice. "I met a crab who taught me to surrender. He said that every time he grew, he left his shell behind and trusted God to provide a new one."

The turtle smiled gently. "God gave me a shell, too. But it's not something I outgrow. It stays with me. And still…it slows me down. I can't move fast. I get flipped easily. I'm vulnerable if I'm not careful."

Colocho frowned. "Why would God give you a shell that's so heavy?"

The turtle turned her eyes toward the horizon. "Because it teaches me not to rush. He knows I'll get where I'm going if I trust His pace."

Before Colocho could respond, the turtle added softly, "Some journeys resist haste. Some voices wait to be heard—until we're quiet enough to notice."

The wind shifted, gentle and cool. Colocho didn't speak again. He simply watched the sky change color, watched the waves roll in their cadence, and realized he had nowhere better to be.

That morning, he learned the second truth of the journey: to grow in faith, he must not always run toward it. Sometimes, he must wait.

Sometimes, he must simply be still.

Colocho…late night…back among the flock…

That night, as stars embroidered the sky, Colocho returned quietly to the pasture. Dew clung to the grass.

Most of the flock had bedded down in the taller reeds, but a few young lambs stirred when he arrived, lifting their heads from the earth.

The same curious lamb who had followed him before stepped forward, blinking sleepily. "Did the sea speak again?"

Colocho nodded slowly. "Not in words. But in its rhythm."

The lamb sat beside him, ears perked. "What did you learn?"

"That the Shepherd doesn't always shout," Colocho whispered. "Sometimes He teaches through stillness. Through the hush. Through waiting."

Another sheep stirred nearby. "But how can we grow if we're not moving?"

Colocho looked up at the stars, then back to them. "Because not all growth is motion. Some roots grow deepest when the surface is still. The turtle taught me that."

The lamb nestled against his side, quiet and thoughtful. "Can you teach us how to wait?"

Colocho blinked, surprised by the question. "I think…I'm still learning myself."

But as he sat with them, he felt something rise within him—gentle, but certain. Their curious eyes reflected no doubt, only anticipation. Awkwardly perfect.

He wasn't just returning anymore. He was beginning to lead.

That had never entered his mind.

Earlier that Evening, on the Other Side of the Day…

The young man was walking the beach as the sun dipped low, casting orange and purple across the waves.

He nearly tripped when he saw the tracks—dozens of tiny flipper marks leading from the dunes to the sea.

Turtle hatchlings.

He followed the tracks back to the nest and quickly called the local turtle rescue hotline. He didn't know how he knew there was a hotline. But somehow, he did.

The young man felt like he'd done something noble today. He chose to help the hatchlings, even though he felt no one was there to help him.

Within the hour, a crew arrived—gentle and efficient, collecting the remaining hatchlings and ensuring their safety.

They worked at an unhurried pace, making sure they got every one of them.

The young man watched as the rescuers moved with love and tenderness. They worked with a care he found himself jealous of.

Among them was an older man who knelt carefully near the nest. As he stood up to leave, a silver cross reflected in the last glows of the sunset.

The glint hit the young man in the eye, and he squinted.

The older man noticed. "We are all God's creatures, and He gave us the responsibility to take care of them."

The young man shrugged, unsure how to respond. He felt like he was just doing what was right.

As the older man lifted the last crate into the back of the truck, his silver necklace snagged on the latch.

It snapped and tumbled—landing silently in the sand near the waves.

Neither man noticed.

The tide crept in unnoticed too, first brushing the edges of the dunes, then sweeping gently across the place where the necklace had fallen.

By the time the young man turned to take one last look at the beach, it was gone.

He didn't know why, but a strange hollowness stirred in his chest, as if something had been lost without his knowing.

Later, when he roamed the sand, he found only driftwood and seaweed. No glint. No chain.

The older man never mentioned it. Perhaps he hadn't realized yet.

But the Shepherd had seen.

And in time, the cross would find its way—washed, hidden, and delivered—to the one who needed it most.

The young man returned to the trailer without anxious energy. Loose. Teeth not hurting.

So he wrote.

Morning Coffee: The First Reflection

The next morning, he stood outside the trailer with coffee in hand. Steam rose into the soft light as the sky turned amber over the water.

He hadn't rushed to wake up. He didn't set an alarm. He just…rose.

The coffee was warm, but not scalding. The air, still touched by night, carried a hush he didn't want to break.

He leaned against the post of the porch and let his body be still.

Yesterday had taught him something. Something subtle. Something real.

"Not everything has to be fixed today," he murmured.

For years, his mornings had started with buzzing—emails, prep lists, deliveries, coffee gulped while lacing his shoes, phone calls in parking lots.

Even on his days off, he couldn't sit still. Rest made him feel useless.

Productivity had become his security blanket…and his prison.

But now?

He watched Colocho move slowly in the pasture. Watched the shadows stretch across the sand. Watched the sea fog rise and dissolve like unspoken prayers.

And for the first time, he didn't feel like a man falling behind.

He just felt…present.

He sipped his coffee and whispered, "Thank You."

And he promised himself—tomorrow, he'd rise again. Coffee in hand. Stillness in heart.

Journal Entry—Unhurried Turtle Time

Found some turtle hatchlings today. The rescuers showed up quickly but they weren't in a rush. No panic. No checklists.

Just patience. They worked like the sun wasn't going anywhere.

Me? I'd have been scrambling to beat the daylight. Trying to fix it before the clock ran out.

An old man with a silver cross talked to me while they worked. Felt like a sermon in disguise.

Why me? I don't know.

But tonight, I'm going to bed without anxiety clawing at my chest.

First time in a while. Feels strange. But good.

I think I'm getting comfortable slowing down.

CHAPTER 4:

A Rattle in the Silence

No Distractions...In the Shadow of the Dunes

COLOCHO AWOKE BEFORE DAWN, DRAWN once again to the beach. The stars still held their place in the sky, and the air felt cooler, quieter. Yet something inside him stirred uneasily, as though the stillness today was thinner—more fragile.

He walked along the familiar path, hooves leaving faint prints in the sand. But as he rounded the bend past a dune, he froze.

Lying in the sand, coiled and unmoving, was a rattlesnake. Its scales glimmered softly in the moonlight, blending seamlessly into the shadows. Only the faint, rhythmic sound of its rattle warned of its presence.

Colocho's breath caught.

The snake did not strike. It watched him silently.

"Why do you make noise if you aren't going to bite?" Colocho asked cautiously, keeping his distance.

The rattlesnake lifted its head slightly, eyes steady. "Not all noise is a threat. Some is a warning. Some is a test."

Colocho stepped back. "I was trying to find peace."

"And instead, you found me," the snake said quietly. "Distraction takes many forms. Some look like danger. Some sound like beauty. Some simply rattle."

Colocho sat down slowly, heart still racing. "Why did God give you a rattle? Other snakes do not have one. It must be hard, living with constant noise."

The snake stopped rattling and hissed softly. "What distracts one can be the very sound another needs to focus."

"Why can't it just be quiet so I can hear God?" Colocho bleated.

"It was," the snake replied. "Until the world filled it."

Colocho noticed other sounds then: wrappers fluttering in the wind, distant music from a camper parked nearby, gulls shrieking overhead.

"I miss the stillness," Colocho whispered.

The rattlesnake slithered away a few feet, then paused. "Find a place the noise cannot reach. Not with louder noise. Not with constant movement. Go where your mind can empty enough to hear again."

Colocho turned from the beach and walked behind a tall dune. Sheltered from the wind and clutter, he lay down quietly. A small piece of the snake's rattle, broken and silent, fell into his wool, cushioned from further noise.

Colocho closed his eyes. At first, the sounds echoed in his mind. But slowly, with each breath, they faded. He focused on the rhythm of the waves, the soft hum of earth beneath him.

And in that silence, something deeper returned—a presence, a whisper, the familiar voice that spoke without sound:

You have found Me, my little sheep.

That morning, Colocho learned the third truth of the journey: to hear the Shepherd's voice, he must clear away distractions. Noise doesn't always shout; sometimes it just rattles. Peace awaits beyond the clamor, in quiet spaces prepared for Him.

Colocho…mid-morning…back at the pasture

Later that morning, Colocho returned to the pasture. As he approached, sheep lifted their heads curiously.

The older ewe stepped forward. "You seem troubled, Colocho. What did you find this morning?"

He paused, collecting his thoughts. "A snake. It rattled loudly but didn't bite."

The younger lambs moved closer, intrigued and slightly fearful.

"It taught me," Colocho continued, "that distractions are everywhere. Some noise can guide, but most just pulls us away from hearing the Shepherd. I learned to seek places beyond the noise—to truly listen."

The lamb nodded thoughtfully. "Then teach us, Colocho. We want to hear the Shepherd clearly, too."

He smiled gently. "Let's find the quiet together."

Later That Night…Fence's edge of the Pasture…

The young man was brushing sand from the collar of his fishing shirt when he noticed Colocho standing near the fence. The sheep's fleece was tangled and tousled from the wind, flecks of sand and dried grass clinging like memories.

The young man jumped when Colocho stepped closer—he could've sworn he heard the dry sound of a rattlesnake. But the sound stopped when the sheep did.

As he reached out to pat him gently, something small and hard dropped from the curls.

He stooped to pick it up: a short, pale segment of a rattlesnake's rattle. It was light as driftwood and hollow, yet something about it felt charged.

He instinctively held it to his ear. This time, there was no whisper like before—only a faint clicking when he shook it. But even that sound pulsed in his chest like a warning…or maybe a reminder.

He stared at it, puzzled.

Colocho looked at him briefly, then resumed grazing. The wind shifted—quiet and low.

The young man tucked the rattle into his coat pocket, beside the crab shell.

He didn't understand what it meant or how it ended up with Colocho.

But he was beginning to expect meaning now. Maybe he wasn't ready for it yet.

And somewhere deep down, he was learning to listen for it.

At the Firepit …

The trailer was still mostly empty—except now, it was slowly filling with items from Colocho's wool. And somehow, those few strange things seemed to hold more meaning than everything else he owned.

He tossed some driftwood into the firepit and lit a match. The flames caught slowly, casting the scent of salt and sea into the night.

Watching the flickering light, his mind began to soften.

He wondered why work and money had always seemed so important. Why his self-worth had revolved around things that faded so quickly. Was working restaurants really where he was supposed to be? Why did he keep spending time—and money—on distractions?

What life should he be living?

What is his purpose?

Morning Coffee: Learning to Listen

At the trailer, the young man sat quietly on the porch steps, coffee steaming between his hands. He stared at the small, hollow piece of rattlesnake rattle resting beside the crab shell on the railing.

Colocho had brought him another unexpected lesson, another quiet clue.

He listened to the distant surf, felt the weight of past distractions—the endless work, the restless chasing. How much had he missed hearing, simply because his life was filled with so much noise?

He breathed deeply, savoring the quiet for the first time in a long while.

"Maybe I've been listening to the wrong things," he whispered.

The sun rose higher, warming his face.

Today, he decided, he would listen differently.

Journal Entry—A Quiet Rattle

Found something else in Colocho's wool today—a rattlesnake rattle. Dry. Hollow.

It didn't whisper, only rattled softly when shaken.

Made me wonder about distractions.

About noise.

About all the things that kept me from listening.

The shell still whispers, but the rattle feels like a reminder—a gentle caution to keep paying attention.

It's different out here.

I'm different out here.

I'm not sure what's changing exactly, but I'm ready to find out.

Maybe the silence is where I finally learn to listen.

CHAPTER 5:

Interlude

The Road Between...Between Loss and Grace

THE SUN HAD ONLY JUST begun to stretch across the pasture when Colocho wandered toward the old highway. The grass along the shoulder was worn down to the root—flattened by time, by tread, by what had been lost there.

He wasn't alone.

A younger lamb followed close, curious and quick-tongued. "I don't know how to do it. To surrender, I mean. I try to stay still, but my thoughts scatter like birds."

Colocho smiled, heart softened by the question. "Stillness isn't something you chase. It finds you. But it begins when you stop running from the Shepherd."

He spoke of the tide. Of the crab. Of quiet mornings and distractions.

Of surrender. Of unhurried time. Of listening when there was no sound at all.

Neither of them noticed the road.

High above, on the ridge where cedar roots held the soil like a thousand knots, a silver-furred wolf stood watch.

His coat was ragged with age, ribs pressing through beneath his skin. But his eyes held depth—like someone who had once been lost but now remembered the way.

He watched the lamb speak. Not with judgment. With hope.

You've learned so much, the wolf thought. *But still… you don't see the road.*

He looked to the asphalt below—black and glinting with morning heat.

He had known this place. It fed his hunger at times.

This road takes things. It does not give them back.

A low rumble grew in the distance.

The lambs didn't hear it.

But he did.

No time.

The engine howled around the bend. A truck surged forward.

The younger lamb froze mid-step, hooves too close to the edge. Colocho turned too late.

Too late.

And so, the wolf ran.

He sprang from the ridge with a force greater than himself.

He did not run for glory.

He ran because he remembered what it was like to be spared.

Let one live, he prayed.

A blur of silver met the road.

Colocho felt it before he understood it—a force slamming into his side, lifting him from the ground. He tumbled into the ditch, dust in his eyes, breath knocked loose.

The truck thundered past.

And then silence.

He blinked, stunned. A soft bleat came from the lamb across the road.

"I'm okay," Colocho whispered, trying to rise. "I'm okay…"

He looked around.

No predator. No protector. Just stillness.

He stared at the sky. "Thank You, Shepherd," he said aloud. "You sent Your hand."

He never saw the wolf.

The young lamb returned to the pasture—safe.

Other side of the road…

On the other side of the road, hidden by the curve of the hill, the wolf lay where the gravel met the earth. Breathing slow. Bones broken. Still watching.

Pain dulled the edges of the world, but his spirit was calm.

He wasn't ready yet, the wolf thought. But maybe…someday, he would be.

He closed his eyes.

And smiled.

CHAPTER 6:

The Image in the Water

Reflecting...In the Tidepool Glass

THE MORNING FOG CLUNG LOW to the earth. Colocho wandered quietly along the shore, the sand cool beneath his hooves. The waves moved in gentle cycles, as if the sea itself were breathing. He was glad he was still breathing. Thankful.

He came upon a shallow pool left behind by the receding tide. The surface shimmered like glass—perfectly still. Colocho leaned in and saw his own reflection.

But he wasn't alone.

Across the pool stood a tall, silver-furred wolf. Its coat shimmered with hints of white and ghostly gray, its eyes a deep amber that seemed to look not just at Colocho—but through him.

Colocho stiffened. "You're a wolf," he said cautiously.

"Yes," the wolf replied calmly. "But wolves do not always hunt."

They stood in silence, the wind whispering around them.

"I've heard stories about wolves," Colocho murmured. "Most end in running or fighting."

The ghost wolf chuckled—a low, hollow sound. "Some stories end that way. But not all. Some are meant for reflection."

He paused, his amber eyes steady. "I've treated others badly. Because that's what wolves are supposed to do. I knew better. But it didn't matter— not until I became the hunted. Only then did I stop long enough to hear His voice—my Creator. Your Shepherd."

He looked out toward the sea. "He forgave me. And I changed. I'm still a wolf…but now I'm a ghost of who I used to be. And that, little one—that is grace."

He turned back to Colocho with a faint, peaceful smile. "I've lived a full life."

Colocho looked down again at the pool, at the mirrored image of himself beside the wolf. "Why are you here?"

"To remember," the wolf said. "To rest."

"To rest?"

The wolf nodded. "I've wandered long, little one. Too long. Some paths led to glory. Others to regret. But always forward. And now…"

He turned his gaze to the dawn breaking over the horizon. "Now I am fulfilling my purpose. I will get to be with Him forever."

Colocho tilted his head. "Who is He?"

The wolf smiled faintly. "Yahweh is the Shepherd's name. He listens. He loves. And He wants to guide you—just as He guided me."

"Will I see you again? Can I go with you?"

"Not like this," the wolf said. "But you will feel me—in the wind, in shadow, in quiet strength when you need it. Because Yahweh may send me."

And with that, the ghost wolf lay beside the pool, eyes closing as golden light washed over his form.

His body shimmered, then faded, like mist touched by morning light. His final breath came quietly, heavy.

Colocho lay alone by the still water, the reflection now showing only himself. As he got up to leave, a silver cross was pulled from the sand and quietly tucked into his wool. The same cross that had glinted in the eye of another. Would it again?

That morning, he learned the fourth truth of the journey: to reflect on his path was not to dwell on the past, but to make peace with it.

Even wolves have stories to tell—some tragic, some triumphant—but all echo the Shepherd's grace. Yahweh's grace.

Colocho stayed most of the day. Before he turned to leave, he noticed the young man in the distance, walking toward the reflection pool.

Colocho watched him in silence, then whispered, "Yahweh."

That Evening, in the Dunes…

The young man wandered the shore after the storm had passed. Driftwood and seaweed were strewn along the path—remnants of something wild and unsettled.

He came to a smooth stretch of sand, where paw and hoof prints intersected—forming a cross.

It seemed intentional. But why?

He stepped carefully around the mark and paused at the reeds, where a silver shape lay slumped beneath.

A wolf. Its fur was salt-crusted, lifeless—but peaceful.

The young man knelt beside it, unsure why his heart ached for something so wild. Something he had once feared.

Then he saw the hoofprints leading away. Colocho had been here.

He sat for a long time, staring out at the horizon, his hands resting in the sand.

He had no words yet. Only a strange stirring.

And softly, reverently, he whispered, "Yahweh."

Back at the Trailer…

The young man looked at the photos on his wall, and a single tear ran down his face. His mind wandered.

Would I die in peace? Would I die without asking for forgiveness? Would I die without saying I'm sorry? Would I die angry?

Where would I go when I die—Heaven? Hell? How do you even get to Heaven…after the life I've lived?

He startled himself.

He hadn't thought about God in a long time. Hadn't thought about death either—at least not like this. Not honestly.

He'd been too busy living. Too busy working. Running from silence. Escaping into noise. Numbing every ache with busyness.

Suddenly, he rushed outside, looked up at the stars, heard the waves crashing, and yelled into the wind, "I need to start over. Now."

He had the revelation that his current situation—his very broken-ness—was the invitation to begin again.

But a question lingered like salt in the air…Would God be in it?

Colocho…That Night, Under the Stars…

Colocho returned to the flock.

The stars above shimmered like pearls in black velvet.

He gathered the lambs beneath the old cedar tree. "I met a wolf," he began, his voice low. "He was once feared. But now…now he walks with Yahweh."

The lambs leaned in, wide-eyed.

"Even wolves can change," Colocho whispered. "Even wolves are loved."

He told them of the pool.

Of reflections.

Of paths.

And of the name—Yahweh.

He glanced at the sand still clinging to his curls. "The crab taught me to surrender. The turtle, to take unhurried steps. To trust the Shepherd's pace, even when the way seems long. The rattlesnake reminded me to turn down the noise and listen again. I didn't see it then. But now I know…The Shepherd was teaching me how to reflect. Because to truly see your path…you need surrender, stillness, and silence."

A lamb tilted its head. "But how do you know where to go?"

Colocho looked out toward the shoreline, eyes soft. "Sometimes, the signs are small. A voice in the waves. A stillness in the wind. And sometimes…"

He paused.

"Sometimes the cross in the sand marks our path—of where we were—because of Him."

"Yahweh."

The Next Morning…

The young man sat on the porch with his coffee. The mug warmed his palms, steam curling in the cool morning air.

He couldn't stop thinking about the wolf. The stillness. The strange peace.

Another sip. Another breath.

"Reflect," he whispered.

He looked out at the pasture. Colocho was already among the flock—gentle, patient, present.

The young man stayed still. And he listened. He reflected.

Journal Entry—Reflection on the Wolf

Found a dead wolf today.

It looked peaceful. That surprised me.

Didn't think something wild could go out like that. Not with peace.

It made me think about my own life. If I keep living like this...how will I go out?

I caught myself thinking: If I looked in the mirror right now, what would I even see?

Not sure. But I don't think I'd like it.

I think I need to start over. Soon.

CHAPTER 7:

A Whisper in the Wind

Quietness...In the Breath of the Dunes

THE BREEZE THAT MORNING CARRIED with it a silence—the kind that made even the gulls pause their cries. Colocho walked alone through the tall grass, still heavy with dew. He had left the pool behind, but the memory of the ghost wolf lingered in his heart like a solemn song.

He wandered inland just slightly, where the dunes formed soft cradles in the earth. And there he saw her.

A great blue heron stood near the edge of another tide pool, balancing carefully on a single long leg. Her wings were folded, her neck drawn tall, and her feathers ruffled gently in the wind.

Colocho paused.

The heron turned her head slowly. "I heard you spoke with the wolf."

Colocho nodded. "He said he was ready to rest."

"He found peace because he believed faithfully," the heron replied. "That is more than many can say."

Colocho stepped closer, noticing the stump where her second leg should have been. "What happened?"

She followed his gaze but did not flinch. "The same wolf, years ago. He was not always old. He was once lost in his hunger, as many are. I survived. Barely. But I did not let it turn me bitter."

"You stayed?" Colocho asked. "Near the same pool?"

"I did," she said. "The world is full of noise—wounds, warnings, words. But here, if you listen long enough, the wind carries something else."

Colocho lowered himself beside her, the silence deepening around them.

"I've been learning about quiet," he said. "Not just the absence of sound. But the kind that makes space to hear what matters."

The heron nodded. "The quiet wasn't empty. It feels like the world is making space…for Someone."

They sat together as the wind stirred the tall grasses, whispering through them like a living prayer.

The heron closed her eyes, one wing lifting slightly in the breeze.

For Colocho, being intentionally quiet was hard to do for long. "Do you ever pray you had both legs again?" Colocho asked softly.

She opened her eyes and looked at him with peace. "I've learned to stand tall on what remains. And that is enough."

The wind shifted, carrying a hush deeper than silence.

Colocho turned to say more, but the heron was no longer there. Only a single blue-gray feather drifted down on him, caught briefly in the breeze before landing gently in his wool.

That morning, Colocho learned the fifth truth of the journey: Intentional quietness is not a retreat—it is an act of faith.

In stillness, wounds are remembered but not reopened. In quiet, Yahweh's voice is clearest.

And as he left the dune, feather tucked gently behind his ear, Colocho heard the wind again. This time, it carried not sorrow, but song.

He often returned to the dunes where he'd met the heron, sitting quietly and listening to the gentle rustle of grass and the wind's quiet song.

He learned to cherish those quiet moments, discovering that silence created space for deeper truths and the Shepherd's reassurance.

Intentional quietness, he realized, opened a clear channel to Yahweh's heart.

That evening, he returned slowly to the pasture, his hooves light in the dew-softened earth.

The younger sheep noticed the feather, but didn't ask.

They simply stepped aside to let him pass, as if they understood.

He stayed silent that night. He just lay beneath the old cedar, the calm wrapped around him—soft, unseen, sure.

And though he said nothing…the flock listened.

The Next Day, with a Fishing Pole and Quiet Hope…

The young man set out in the early afternoon, carrying a simple fishing pole and a small tackle box.

He wandered down to a nearby jetty, where the tide rolled lazily against the rocks. He cast his line and waited.

And waited.

Hours passed. The sun arced across the sky. Waves lapped gently, but no fish tugged at his line.

A part of him felt foolish—he'd hoped, for some reason, that today would be different. *Maybe I should pray for a fish.*

Just as the sky began to deepen with the colors of dusk, he packed up and stood to leave.

That's when he heard the rush of wings.

A heron flew low overhead, gliding in gracefully. It banked slightly, and as it did, something slipped from its beak—a fish, glinting silver in the last light of the day.

It landed just a few feet in front of the young man.

He stared at it, stunned. Not because it was large or special— but because it was there, dropped from the sky like a gift.

He knelt and gently picked it up, still cool and damp in his hands.

Above him, the heron circled once, then disappeared into the horizon.

The young man didn't smile or speak. He just looked at the fish, then up at the sky, and breathed out slowly.

Grateful. To a God he had not spoken to—and now, he wondered if that God had just answered a prayer he hadn't even known he was praying. Maybe, deep in his heart…he had.

That Same Evening, Just Beyond the Pasture…

The young man returned to his trailer—fish in hand, mind still turning.

He cleaned it slowly, carefully, as if it were something priceless.

He was saving the propane for something like this.

The flames flickered gently—not in urgency, but welcome.

The fish sizzled on the rusty old grill—now clean, reclaimed.

He flipped it effortlessly. Cooked to perfection.

He sat cross-legged in the dirt, firelight flickering across his face, and ate every bite in silence.

Not out of ritual, but reverence.

The heron's gift felt like more than a meal.

It tasted like a whisper: *You are seen.*

Morning Coffee: The Sound of Silence

The next morning, the young man woke without an alarm. Just breath. And light.

He stepped outside barefoot, coffee in hand, and sat on the trailer step.

The breeze was soft, tugging at the edges of his flannel shirt.

Somewhere nearby, sheep moved through the pasture like slow ideas.

He didn't check the time. He stayed silent.

He just…listened. To the wind. To the rustle of the grass. To the quiet that no longer felt empty, but expectant.

He thought of the heron. Of the fish. Of the prayer he hadn't spoken out loud—but maybe had whispered in his heart.

And as the steam rose upward like incense, he breathed out slowly and said, "Thank You."

Not because he had answers. But because God had met him in the silence.

Journal Entry—The Fish I Didn't Ask For

I went fishing today. Didn't catch a thing. Waited for hours. Felt stupid for hoping. Felt more stupid for almost praying.

Right when I was about to leave, a heron dropped a fish out of the sky.

No joke. Like it was meant for me.

I picked it up. Cooked it. Ate it by the fire. Didn't even season it.

It tasted...beyond my expectation. Special. Like grace, maybe.

I don't know what to do with that. But I said "thank You" to a God I haven't talked to in years.

Maybe I did pray. Just didn't know it.

Either way...He answered.

CHAPTER 8:

One Step Back...One Step Forward

Regret and Grace...In the Glow of the Firepit

THAT EVENING, HE REACHED OUT.

Not in a grand way—just a few messages. A photo of the sunrise. A text to his family. A few old friends. Even his ex-fiancée.

Hope you're doing well.

Simple. Soft. Nothing dramatic.

But beneath each word was a quiet ache: *I'm sorry. I miss you. I'm trying.*

He waited.

One thumbs-up came back. That was all.

The rest sat unanswered, floating in the gray space between hope and history.

He stared at the screen until it dimmed in his hand.

Then, without saying a word—even to himself—he walked to the fire pit.

That night, the fire was more for company than warmth. The young man sat alone beside a shallow ring of stones, the kindling crackling beneath a layer of driftwood. Stars blinked above—soft, distant. His breath came slow in the dark.

Beside him, half-buried in the sand, was a bottle he hadn't seen in months—dug out from an old crate during the move. He hadn't meant to grab it. Wasn't even sure why he did.

Just one sip. Then another.

Not to celebrate. Not to rebel. Just to dull the silence that had grown too large for the room.

The fire hissed and shifted. He stared into it like it might answer him. But all it gave was heat and flickers.

The bottle wasn't empty when he set it down, but it was too empty for comfort.

His body slouched forward, heavier than before. He wasn't drunk—at least not fully. But his thoughts scattered like ash. His soul felt swollen with the ache of a question he still didn't know how to ask.

"Are You even real?" he muttered toward the flame.

No thunder. No echo. Just the pop of sap and wood curling into itself.

He wiped his face with both hands and dragged himself back to the trailer.

When he laid down, the room tilted slightly. The world didn't spin, but it swayed.

And somewhere between guilt and sleep, he whispered, "Sorry," to no one in particular.

Morning Coffee: Quiet Regret

The next morning, the coffee tasted bitter—and not just because the grounds were cheap.

He sat on the step outside the trailer, mug warming his hands.

His head ached faintly, but not from the drink. From the knowing.

The fire pit still held last night's embers. Cold now. Hollow.

He looked out at the pasture. Colocho was there, moving slowly along the fence line, same as every morning.

Calm. Purposeful.

But he didn't feel calm. He felt…cracked. Not broken. Just hairline fractured in ways he thought had healed.

He hadn't drunk to feel good. He drank to feel nothing.

But nothing doesn't stay quiet for long. It echoes. And it regrets.

He sighed and took another sip. Steam curled like a thought unfinished.

"I'm sorry," he whispered. Then added, even softer, "Thank You...for not walking away."

He stared at Colocho's wool catching the light like memory. The lamb didn't judge. Just grazed.

He sat inside the quiet—not to run from the noise, but to find what lived beyond it.

Maybe grace wasn't loud. Maybe it was this: A dawn that still came. A sheep that still stayed. A God who still listened.

And a second chance he didn't ask for, but received anyway.

Later That Day...

He wandered toward the marina, unsure why. Something in him stirred to take a long walk.

As he approached, he noticed an older man untangling nets by the dock. His hands were sun-darkened and knotted like driftwood. A small red cooler sat beside him. Two pelicans eyed it hungrily from the posts.

"You fish?" the man asked, without looking up.

"Only once," the young man said. "Didn't catch a thing."

The man chuckled. "That's how most of us start."

He smiled and watched in silence. The quiet between them wasn't awkward. It was peaceful.

After a moment, he told the story of the heron and the fish.

The fisherman paused, then nodded slowly. "Sometimes we ask without asking. God still hears." He stood, stretched, and looked him over. "You looking for work?"

He blinked. "Actually…I think I might be."

"We're short a dock hand. Work's early, but honest. You'll smell like salt and sweat most days. But if you don't mind your hands getting tired—there's a place for you."

He looked out at the water, where the heron had flown, and something in his chest loosened. "I'd like that."

And just like that, without striving or a résumé, he was hired.

Not because he pushed. But because he paused.

Because he had been quiet enough…to listen.

Journal Entry—Didn't Deserve It, Got It Anyway

I messed up last night. I wasn't trying to fall back. I just didn't want to feel...anything.

The bottle wasn't full, but it was full enough. And I knew better.

Didn't drink to celebrate. Didn't drink to forget. Just drank to mute the noise inside my chest.

But it didn't work. It never does. Just leaves me feeling more hollow than before.

And still...

This morning, the sun came up. Coffee still brewed. Colocho and the others still grazed.

And somehow...God still listened.

Grace showed up in silence. Again.

Then later...I got a job offer I didn't ask for. Didn't earn. Didn't even expect.

It felt like God saying, "I saw that. All of it. And I'm still here."

I don't deserve a second chance. But I got one.

So I'll take it. And this time...I'll try not to waste it.

CHAPTER 9:

Word in the Sky

The Word...Written in the Clouds

THE NIGHT HAD BROUGHT A storm—wind howled with the cry of wild creatures, scared and hungry, calling out to the darkness. Rain lashed across the pasture, bending the grass low and filling every hollow with water. Colocho slept fitfully in the shelter of a dune, curled beneath the drifting feathers of the great blue heron's memory.

At dawn, silence returned. Colocho stepped carefully outside, blinking against the soft light that broke through scattered clouds. The sand, freshly swept by the tide, gleamed golden under his hooves.

And there, written in the drifting clouds, were pictures—faint outlines, but somehow, they spoke to Colocho's heart. Shapes of a path, a flame, and a shepherd's staff all gently swirling together like breath.

Then, the words came. Not aloud, but deep within, undeniable. *My word will be the glow beneath your hooves. Where you step, I will light the way.*

Colocho's breath caught. He stood still, waves lapping nearby, as the verse etched itself into his soul. He had heard the Shepherd's voice in waves, in wind, in quiet… and now, unmistakably, in His Word.

Colocho…as the sun peeked…beneath the wide sky…

He turned and began the walk back to the pasture, the verse echoing in his spirit. When he arrived, the old gruff sheep was watching from atop the hill.

His eyes narrowed as Colocho approached. But then they caught something—light, reflecting from Colocho's wool. The old sheep leaned forward. "What is that?" he asked, not unkindly.

Colocho turned slightly. A silver necklace had become tangled in his curls, and at its center hung a small silver cross.

The old sheep's eyes widened, softening. "A cross," he murmured. "Haven't seen one of those since…well, a long time." He motioned for Colocho to sit.

"You've changed," the elder said. "Where have you been?"

"Listening," Colocho replied. "Learning."

The old sheep sighed deeply. "Then it's time you heard our story— the story of the sheep and the others." His voice became low, steady, like a song passed down through generations.

"In the beginning, the Shepherd created us. We roamed green fields and followed His voice. Then the world grew dark, and people strayed. But God spoke, and they used unblemished lambs as sacrifices for all their evil. Yet even after hundreds of years, man continued to sin. So God's Son came—to be the final sacrifice. He was named Jesus, the Lamb of God."

Colocho's eyes widened. "The lamb…died for others?"

"Yes," the old sheep said. "To give one's life for another is the greatest act of love. I was just a lamb myself in a school play once. I heard the story of a child born in a manger—God's Son, in human form. How He became the Good Shepherd. How He left the ninety-nine to find the one who was lost."

The old sheep's voice trembled. "But people turned on Him. They nailed Him to a cross. But He wasn't done—not even death could hold Him. On the third day, He returned. He had taken all our sins—yours, mine, theirs. No more sacrifices. Only faith."

Tears welled in Colocho's eyes. A deep warmth spread through his chest. "So… we just have to believe?" he whispered.

The old sheep nodded. "Almost—ask for forgiveness and believe, and by His grace, we're welcomed into heaven."

Colocho raised his head toward the morning sky, breath catching in his throat. And then, from somewhere deep inside, he let out a single, strong bleat: "Yahweh."

It rang over the pasture and drifted on the wind. In that moment, Colocho understood—he had been calling out all along. In fear, in joy, in pain…he had been calling the name above all names. The name that had heard him every step of the way.

Colocho…That Afternoon, a Flock Listening…

That day, he stood before the younger sheep, gathered around the hilltop, and shared what he had seen in the sky.

"The Shepherd is speaking," he told them. "Not just in the waves or the wind, but in His Word. It's written for us, and it shines a path. Each verse is a step forward or a reflection"

And the flock began to listen differently after that.

CHAPTER 10:

Called by Name

Identity...In the Shepherd's Voice

THE SUN WAS JUST BEGINNING to rise as the young man stepped outside with his coffee. Colocho stood at the edge of the pasture, his curls catching the first light of day.

Drawn by some quiet pull, the young man walked toward him.

Colocho didn't move away—only looked up with calm, steady eyes.

The young man reached down, gently patting his side. His fingers brushed against something cool and metallic, buried deep in the wool. Carefully, he pulled it free.

It was a silver cross—small, worn, simple. The chain was tangled, as if it had been carried for some time.

He held it in his palm and stared. It was the same one the turtle rescue worker had lost weeks ago. How had it ended up here?

He looked at Colocho again. The sheep's gaze met his, still and unwavering.

Then Colocho let out a soft, breathy bleat. "Yahweh."

The young man felt something stir deep in his chest—a warmth, a stillness, a call. Without a word, he turned and walked quickly back to his trailer.

Inside, he knelt by an old cardboard box, digging until he found what he was looking for: a Bible.

He opened it. Inside the front cover was a faded note, written in his grandmother's familiar hand: *To Jude—Never forget whose you are. Love, Grandma.*

He stared at the name. Jude. His real name.

The one he hadn't heard in years. The one he'd tucked away beneath nicknames and jokes and distractions. The one he was ready to claim.

He flipped to a page marked by an old bulletin. A verse was highlighted—Isaiah 43:1. *Fear not, for I have redeemed you; I have called you by name, you are mine.*

He held the cross against his chest. He didn't say anything aloud. But something in him said yes.

That Night, by the Fire Pit…

Jude sat alone beside the fire. Its light flickered against his face, dancing shadows across the worn leather of his journal.

In his hand, he held the silver cross. It shimmered in the glow—not polished, not perfect, but whole. Just like him.

He turned it over slowly and whispered aloud, not to the fire, but through it.

"Jude." He let the name settle into the space around him. "I always thought it was too quiet."

He paused. "They used to sing that song—'Hey Jude.' Thought I needed something tougher."

The fire cracked gently.

"But Grandma wrote it. In the Bible. Not just because it was mine… but because it was already His."

He looked up at the stars, his voice barely above breath.

"It's time to stop hiding."

He didn't say anything else.

He didn't have to.

The fire spoke in warmth, the sky in peace, and his name—finally his own—echoed softly in his soul.

The Following Morning…

 Morning came again without alarm or hurry.

Jude stepped outside, barefoot again, coffee in hand. The mug warmed his palms. The air smelled of dew and salt and something still.

In the distance, Colocho stood at the edge of the pasture, facing the sunrise.

Jude didn't move toward him. He just watched—then sat down slowly on the step.

And from the quiet of his heart, he spoke the name that had been rising in him for days:

"Yahweh."

There was no miracle in that moment.

Just peace. And that was perfect.

Journal Entry—Carried in the Wool

I found a cross today. Not in a drawer. Not in the dirt. In a sheep's wool. That shouldn't make sense. But somehow, it does.

I held it, and it felt like it had been traveling for me. Like it had waited until I was ready to take it back.

I sat with it by the fire. Let it glow. Let it remind me.

I used to hate my name. Jude. Too soft. Too poetic. The Beatles didn't help. So I hid behind JJ. Hid from myself.

But tonight, I held the name like I held the cross—Not just as something I inherited. But something I've been called back to.

Maybe it wasn't weak. Maybe it was sacred. Maybe…it was His idea all along.

Yahweh called me by name. And I finally heard it.

CHAPTER 11:

Dancing in the Dawn

Grace...In the First Steps of Light

THE NEXT MORNING, COLOCHO WOKE before the sun had even thought to rise. The air was cool and still, and the pasture lay quiet beneath a velvet sky. But something in him stirred—not restlessness, but resolve.

The memory of the Word in the sky still warmed him.

He was no longer just a lost sheep. No longer just learning. Now— he was leading.

As he reached the familiar shoreline, he noticed something—small, trembling, caught in the sand.

A young lamb. It was shivering, frightened, and unsure. Its cries were soft, barely more than whimpers. Colocho approached slowly, gently. He knew this fear. He had lived it. He had cried on this very sand once.

"It's okay," Colocho whispered. "You're not alone."

The lamb looked up, its eyes wide. Colocho pressed his forehead to the lamb's and guided it out of the soft sand to firmer ground.

As they walked back toward the pasture, Colocho looked over his shoulder at the beach. He had an idea. No, not an idea. A calling.

He turned to the lamb. "Would you like to come back here tomorrow?" The lamb nodded slowly, unsure though.

Colocho…That Evening, Among the Flock…

As the sky faded into twilight, Colocho didn't lie down with the rest of the flock. Instead, he moved from one corner of the pasture to the next, visiting small groups of sheep.

"You don't have to believe yet," he told them gently. "Just come and see. Meet me at the beach tomorrow. Before dawn."

Some blinked at him, unsure. Others whispered among themselves. A few nodded quietly. One by one, hearts began to open.

He paused under the old cedar tree, looking toward the stars as they scattered across the deepening blue. "I wasn't always Colocho," he said softly, more to himself than to the flock. "A human gave me that name. Said it meant curls. I used to think that was all I was—just the sheep with the wild wool."

He looked down at the little lamb beside him.

"But maybe…the name came from the Shepherd. Maybe it was always meant for me. And maybe yours is already waiting too."

That Same Evening, on the Other Side of the Fence…

Just before sunset, Jude walked to the fence line out of habit. He didn't expect anything—just wanted to see Colocho and the others again. A small, quiet part of him hoped to catch a glimpse of the one with curls.

And there he was.

Colocho waited in the center of the pasture, moving slowly from one cluster of sheep to the next. He wasn't grazing. He was bleating—not in fear, not in alarm, but softly, as if calling. Gathering.

The other sheep lifted their heads. Some followed. Some hesitated. A few stayed where they were, but watched.

Behind Colocho, close to his back legs, a tiny lamb stood trembling—its coat still damp, its legs wobbly. It clung to Colocho's side like it had nowhere else to go.

Jude leaned against the fence, heart quiet. He remained still. Didn't call out. He simply took it in.

Colocho continued to walk slowly through the flock, the little lamb trailing behind him like a shadow. And the strangest thing—the most peculiar thing—was how the others began to fall in step. Not all at once. But one by one. As if they trusted him. As if they knew.

Jude didn't say a word. But his hand rested on the cross at his chest. A memory, sharp and clear, washed over him—the voice of his grandmother, the weight of her Bible, the smell of cedar and old pages.

Something broke inside him. Not a wound—a wall.

He dropped to his knees in the sand by the fence, unable to hold it in any longer. His voice cracked under the weight of truth.

"I've done things I don't talk about. I've treated people badly. I've lived like God didn't matter. Like I didn't matter. God, please…forgive me."

There were no theatrics. No thunderclap. Just a breeze through the grass, and a warmth in his chest that hadn't been there in years.

Colocho…That Night…Under the stars…

Colocho lay atop a small hill above the pasture, the stars scattered above like quiet promises. The flock rested below, the little lamb curled at his side.

He breathed in deeply, letting the cool wind brush his curls.

"Thank You," he whispered to the Shepherd. "For finding me. For staying with me. For letting me lead others to You."

And with the feather still tucked behind his ear, Colocho closed his eyes— Not in weariness, But in prayer.

Meanwhile, Down by the Marina…

Jude wiped the salt from his sleeves as he helped the marina owner secure the last cleat. The ropes creaked softly against the dock, the tide sloshing like a tired lullaby.

The owner reached into his pocket and tossed Jude a set of tarnished keys. "1972 Chevy. She's rough. But she runs. Found her on blocks behind the fish shed. She's yours—if you'll take her."

Jude stared at the keys in his hand, chipped paint flaking from the ring. He brushed them against the silver cross at his chest and swallowed hard. "I…I can't take it," he said quietly. "I don't deserve it. Didn't earn it."

The owner met his eyes without flinching. "Yet you get it anyway. That's how faith works."

Silence settled between them. The sun dipped lower over the harbor, casting long shadows across the dock.

"Thanks, boss," Jude whispered.

He chuckled, shaking his head. "Stop calling me boss. Call me Peter." He leaned on the piling and let out a breath. "I've hauled nets through hurricanes, watched men drown in their regrets. Seen grace show up as a rope, a raft…sometimes as rust and four wheels."

Jude's laugh cracked open the quiet. "My name's Jude," he said. "No more JJ."

Peter paused, then smiled. "Jude, huh?" He began humming under his breath. "Hey Jude…"

They both laughed. Then they shook on it—old grace meeting new steps.

Jude flipped the keys once more in his palm, then loaded his rusty bike into the truck bed.

The Next Morning…

Coffee steamed in the cup Jude held as he sat on the tailgate of his newly gifted pickup, now parked near the edge of the pasture. The ocean breeze tugged at the loose collar of his shirt.

He could see Colocho again—standing in the same spot near the hill, facing the rising light.

Jude reached for his journal and wrote.

Journal Entry—Still Breathing

I used to chase everything.

 Money. Approval. Escape. I even chased the sunrise...like it could fix something in me.

But this morning, I'm still. Just watching light spill over the pasture. No need to earn it. No need to deserve it.

God doesn't rush healing. He just keeps showing up.

Like Colocho. Like the cross. Like the heron.

And this name—Jude.

 I used to run from it. Now I'm walking in it.

I'm still breathing. Still learning. Still found.

CHAPTER 12:

The Dawn Revival

Enjoying God...In the Chorus of the Sea

IT HAD BEEN MANY FULL moons since the last gathering. Colocho remembered it—the songs, the baptisms, the stillness that wrapped around the waves like a holy current. Since then, he had returned each morning, not out of habit, but out of hope. He didn't look for crowds. He listened for the Shepherd.

And now...they had returned.

From the ridge, Colocho saw the humans arriving in darkness—lifting tents, strumming quiet chords, forming a wide circle facing the sea. The air held a profound hush, as if even the stars had paused their shining to watch. Faint guitar strings floated into the wind, fragile and faithful.

At first light, Colocho stepped forward.

He moved softly over the dunes, the flock following behind him. Some were unsure. Some were ready. But they followed—not because they were told, but because something deeper called. A gentle urgency tugged at their hearts. They were being drawn, not driven.

On the shore, the humans began to sing. A low hum at first—then voices lifted with the rising sun.

Then, through the mist, Colocho and the others appeared.

At the head of the flock walked Colocho, his wool catching the morning light like silver fire. His steps were slow, deliberate, steady. The wind shifted as the first light broke over the sea, and Colocho paused at the top of the dune.

He felt the pull to move forward—but just for a moment, he stayed still.

The waves called gently. The flock waited behind him, uncertain but watching.

And Colocho—he closed his eyes.

This was not fear. Not hesitation. It was reverence.

He remembered his first time standing on this beach, hooves unsure, heart trembling, waves rushing in with questions he didn't know how to ask. Back then, he had been alone—except for the Shepherd's whisper. Back then, he didn't know his name.

Now he did.

He heard it again. Not shouted, but spoken softly from within.

Colocho.

The name was not just curls and wool. It was a calling. A mantle. A reminder that even sheep could be chosen. Even sheep could lead.

He opened his eyes.

Down below, the voices rose in worship. The young lamb stood beside him, breathing fast but standing firm. Behind her, others gathered in small clusters.

They didn't follow because he was perfect.

They followed because he had stayed.

Because he had returned.

Because he kept listening.

Colocho breathed in the salty air, nodded once to the dawn, and took the first step.

The sand shifted beneath him—but his spirit didn't.

He was steady.

And as the tide reached for his legs, he whispered not to the sea, but to the Shepherd, "Let them hear You…even if they follow me."

The water touched his chest. The lambs followed. And Colocho walked into the waves not as one seeking salvation, but as one showing the way to it. The tide welcomed him. And the lambs followed. One by one. Calm. Steady. Trusting.

Some paused at the water's edge. Others walked in without hesitation. The flock moved as one body—uncertain, yet unafraid. As they stood in the surf, the waves rolled over their legs, and the light broke fully across the sea.

A quiet gasp rippled through the crowd. But no one moved. No one spoke.

And for a moment, the sea and the song and the silence all became one. It was not planned. It was not rehearsed. It was holy.

CHAPTER 13:

The Baptism

The Morning...Of Water and New Life

THE YOUNG MAN—JUDE—WOKE before dawn, his chest stirring with something unnamed. He stepped barefoot into the cool grass and followed the path without thinking. He didn't grab his journal. He didn't take his coffee. He simply walked—toward the beach, toward the light, toward something greater.

When he reached the dune, he stopped—and dropped to his knees.

Before him, Colocho and the others were walking into the water. Beside them, humans sang and wept and worshipped. No one led from a stage. No one held a microphone. The Spirit was doing the leading. And at the center of it all stood Colocho—still, certain, shining.

Jude clutched the cross around his neck. The same one he had once found tangled in Colocho's wool. Back then, it had been a curiosity. Now, it was a conviction.

A figure knelt beside him—an older man, shoulders weathered by wind and work. His eyes were glassy as they locked onto the cross.

"I lost that," the man said softly. "Weeks ago. Didn't even know when it fell. Just…gone."

Jude looked down, heart pounding. "It found its way back."

"I remember you. The night we saved the hatchlings. I never got your name."

Jude stood slowly, looking to the older man. "My name is Jude," he said, voice firm and free. "And I'm ready."

From the edge of the beach, another voice joined them—Peter's. Familiar, yet gentler now.

Together, the marina owner and the turtle rescuer stepped into the water with him. No title. No ceremony. Just faith. Just grace.

They lowered him into the sea.

And when he rose, he gasped—not for air, but because he was breathing again. Truly breathing.

After the Baptism…

Water still dripped from Jude's face as he waded back to shore. He wasn't sure what to say—how to speak after something that changed everything. But the two men who had lowered him into the sea stood waiting.

Not with applause.

Just presence.

The older one, the fisherman, offered a towel. "You alright, son?"

Jude nodded, breath still catching. "More than alright."

He looked between them. "You two know each other?"

The fisherman chuckled. "We've known of each other. But never really met." He extended a weathered hand. "Peter."

The quiet man beside him clasped his hand with warmth. "Joel."

Jude froze for a moment, then let out a slow, quiet breath. "Of course it is."

Peter raised a brow. "What's that mean?"

Jude just shook his head, grinning through the saltwater and grace. "Yahweh is God."

Joel smiled softly. "Always has been."

Peter clapped Jude gently on the back, his hand firm and kind. "Never thought I'd be part of something like this," he said, voice rough with emotion. "I'm just a fisherman."

Jude glanced toward the dunes, still smiling. "He owns the marina," he added, half-joking but full of warmth.

Peter shrugged, brushing a hand through his damp hair. "Some days, I still just feel like the kid who used to cast nets before sunrise."

They stood there, three men, ankle-deep in the dawn. No one rushed away. No one checked the time.

Jude looked out toward the sea, then back to the pasture.

"It feels like home."

Peter slapped Jude on the back again, his voice carrying a quiet joy. "Well, welcome to the light, son."

And They Ate Together…

Later that morning, barefoot and still damp, Jude followed Peter and Joel up the sandy path behind the dunes to a small wooden building that clung to the edge of the church lot like a seashell that refused to blow away.

Inside, the air smelled of coffee and cinnamon rolls. Someone had cracked open the windows, letting the sea breeze mingle with the warmth of breakfast.

They didn't say much at first.

Plates were filled. Coffee poured. They found a plastic table near the corner, its legs uneven but faithful, and sat on folding chairs that creaked in protest beneath weathered weight and new beginnings.

Peter buttered a biscuit with slow, deliberate strokes. Joel said grace with a quiet voice and a bowed head. Jude just sat—towel draped around his neck, hands wrapped around a chipped mug like it might float away if he let go.

The silence wasn't awkward.

It was full.

Finally, Jude cleared his throat. "I keep seeing this sheep."

Peter looked up. "Sheep?"

"Yeah," Jude said, almost sheepishly. "Curly wool. Calm eyes. Shows up near the fence most mornings. Sometimes on the beach. Sometimes it's like…like he's listening to something I can't hear."

Joel raised an eyebrow. "You gave him a name?"

"Colocho," Jude said with a slight grin. "Means *curly* in Spanish."

Peter chuckled, tearing his biscuit in half. "I once had a goat show up to a Sunday service. Sat in the aisle for half the sermon. Never looked more convicted."

Joel sipped his coffee, then leaned back. "Strange how God works. Sometimes He sends ravens to prophets. Sometimes whales to prodigals. Sometimes…maybe sheep to the tired."

Jude nodded slowly, eyes down. "I thought I was chasing the sunrise. But lately, I think it was chasing me."

Joel studied him a moment, then smiled—not with amusement, but recognition. "You know the story. The Shepherd leaves the ninety-nine to go after the one."

"Yeah," Jude replied softly. "I've always loved that story."

Peter leaned forward, fork pointing gently toward Jude's chest. "Sounds to me like, in your case…the ninety-nine followed the one."

Jude looked up.

Joel nodded slowly. "Just to make sure you got home."

The room went quiet again—but not empty. It hummed with something sacred.

Jude blinked back the salt in his eyes, unsure if it came from the sea or the grace.

Then, almost in a whisper, he said, "I think He sent Colocho."

Peter smiled. "Seems like the Shepherd's been sending him all along."

They didn't speak much more after that. They didn't need to.

The breakfast was simple. The fellowship holy.

And the sunrise, now fully risen, poured through the windows like an unspoken blessing.

Colocho Returns to the Pasture…

Colocho walked among the flock, his wool still damp from the day before. The heron feather was now woven more tightly into his curls—like it belonged there.

He moved slowly, greeting each sheep. The young lamb from the beach ran to him and pressed its head to his shoulder.

"You stayed with me," the lamb whispered. "Even when I was scared."

Colocho nodded. "That's what the Shepherd does. And now…that's what I do."

Around him, murmurs rose among the flock.

"What was that yesterday?"

"Why did you go into the water?"

"Why did the people sing when we arrived?"

Colocho gathered them beneath the old cedar tree. "It was a revival. A coming back. For them. For us."

"Why now?" asked a skeptical ewe. "Why after all this time?"

Colocho looked toward the ridge, where the morning light was still climbing. "Because the Shepherd never stops calling. And eventually…the lost stop running."

The flock grew quiet. The lambs huddled close.

"Will we go again?" one asked.

"Yes," Colocho said, a smile rising in his eyes. "But not just to be washed. Next time…to lead others there."

Colocho…Under the Old Cedar Tree…

Late in the morning, Colocho gathered the flock beneath the old cedar tree, its branches now familiar with their rhythm of return.

The lambs huddled close, the older sheep forming a loose circle. They had followed him into the waves, but now they had questions. Not of doubt, but of longing.

A young lamb spoke first. "Why do you listen for the Shepherd? Even when we can't see Him?"

Colocho paused, his gaze lifting toward the ridge where the sun had first broken. "Because His voice found me before I knew I was lost."

Another asked, "What if we can't always hear Him?"

"You will," Colocho said softly. "Maybe not as thunder. Maybe not even as words. But the Shepherd's voice feels like peace…even in the middle of fear. You'll know, because it won't sound like shame. It'll sound like home."

A third sheep—one who had watched from the edge of the pasture for weeks—stepped forward. "But why should we follow? What if it's easier just to stay safe?"

Colocho looked at them, his voice firm now, but tender. "I used to stay safe. I stayed behind fences that weren't even locked. I told myself the Shepherd would come to me—but I never moved toward Him. But the Shepherd didn't just call me to be safe. He called me to be whole. And when I followed…I found who I really was."

Silence fell again—not the awkward kind, but the sacred kind.

Then, with the breeze stirring the cedar leaves above them, Colocho said, "If you follow Him, you'll find pastures you've never dreamed of. You'll walk through storms and still sing. You'll lose some things you thought you needed—but you'll find the One who never left."

The lambs leaned in, hearts full and eyes wide.

He wasn't just a sheep anymore.

He was becoming their shepherd.

The Next Morning…

Jude sat on the tailgate of his old truck, parked just above the pasture line. A fresh cup of coffee steamed between his palms. His journal sat beside him, closed for now. The only writing he needed was the dawn painting gold across the horizon.

He looked toward the pasture. Colocho and the others grazed peacefully. The breeze stirred their wool like a benediction. And there was Colocho—standing on the ridge again. Watching the sky. Listening.

Jude smiled softly. Not everything needed fixing. Not everything needed understanding. Some things just needed presence.

He bowed his head. "Thank You, Yahweh. For Colocho and the others. For the sea. For the cross. For the dawn that came even when I didn't ask."

CHAPTER 14:

The Endless Dawn

Eternal Light...Rising Beyond the Shore

A MONTH HAD PASSED SINCE the revival, and the mornings had settled into their rhythm again. The world had returned to its ordinary heartbeat—But something inside Colocho had not.

He looked out over the waves as the sun rose again. It was not just beautiful—it was true. Each dawn reminded him.

He no longer feared the ocean. Or the unknown. Or the future.

He had learned to surrender. To be still. To listen. To trust.

He heard the Shepherd's voice once more. Not from the horizon, not from thunder or wind, but from within.

You are ready.

The dawn had become more than a time of day. It was the rhythm of his soul. It was how he walked, breathed, led, and loved. Not as a lamb seeking refuge, but as a shepherd echoing the Shepherd.

Fully transformed, Colocho no longer wandered. He walked with purpose. With peace.

And as he stood at the water's edge, surrounded by sheep and those who walked the path with him, he knew: He was no longer the one being found. He was leading others home. He was a shepherd for the Shepherd.

The New Dawn…

Light crested over the waves like it had every morning, Yet this one felt different.

Jude stood barefoot in the surf, his jeans soaked to the knees, the cross pressed gently against his chest—

the same cross he once found by accident. The same one that had marked his return.

He stayed silent. Didn't sing. He just stood still and soaked in the presence of God.

The dawn wasn't just light. It was a promise. It was peace.

Behind him, Colocho waited still, the sea breeze gently tugging at his wool. The man turned, and their eyes met. Colocho held his gaze. Then slowly turned and began walking away. Not out of rejection, but invitation.

It was Jude's turn now. To walk. To stay. To lead.

He looked down at the footprints beside his own. Some were his, others were Colocho's. But one set—deeper, stronger—had always walked by his side.

He closed his eyes and heard it again. Not in his ears but in his heart:

You are ready.

The word wasn't a command. It was a confirmation.

He was no longer just a seeker. He was found. And he was becoming.

From that day forward, every moment he lived carried the rhythm of the dawn.

Yahweh. The name he once whispered in confusion was now the name he carried in joy.

The sun rose. And it would never set the same way again.

CHAPTER 15:

The Lamb That Stayed

Faithfulness...More than a Shadow

THE BEACH WAS QUIET AGAIN. The songs had faded. The tents had long been packed away. But one small lamb remained.

She stood at the edge of the sea, the surf licking gently at her hooves, watching the sun stretch across the water.

She didn't come for signs. She came for the whisper.

No one had seen Colocho for days—maybe even weeks. Some believed he'd gone inland, called to lead others. Some said he still came before dawn, leaving only hoofprints too soft to last.

But the lamb didn't mind.

She remembered the way Colocho had stood there. Not for display, but for direction. He had watched the dawn like it was a letter from God, not just a light.

One morning, she remembered the lesson of Surrendering to the gentle waves. She stepped closer to the water, letting the tide carry her hooves briefly, whispering a simple prayer of trust.

Another morning, she lay still on the sand for Unhurried Time, Watching the sky slowly shift from indigo to gold. She didn't rush it. She let the morning speak first.

Later, when the beach became crowded with gulls and rustling wind, she wandered behind the dune, honoring the lesson of No Distractions. And there, in the stillness, the Shepherd's voice was clearer than ever.

Some days, she would pause by a tide pool and see her own reflection—remembering to Reflect on Her Path. She saw her scars. Her healing. Her belonging.

Each dawn taught her anew. Intentional Quietness shaped her into a listener, a worshiper of whispers, not shouts.

One morning, she saw the words traced gently in the clouds:

He tends to His flock like a shepherd. He gathers the lambs in His arms and carries them close to His heart.

The Shepherd's Words of the Day. Not written in pages, but in sky.

And one morning, she danced. She danced in the dawn, splashing in the water with joy,

the lesson of Enjoying Time with God written not in books, but in breath.

EPILOGUE:

The Endless Sunrise

After Surrender... After Dawn

THE LAMB RETURNED EACH MORNING. She didn't try to lead. She just listened.

And in time, others joined her. Not because she called. But because something gentle pulled at their hearts. First one. Then two. Then five.

They didn't always know why they came. Only that it felt right to be there when the sun rose.

One morning, the lamb found something nestled in the sand—a single feather. Blue-gray. Rimmed with light.

She tucked it behind her ear, just as Colocho once had.

Another day, she spotted faint hoofprints beside her own. They were washed quickly by the tide, but they had been there.

She smiled.

She stood taller now—not quite a shepherd, but no longer a lamb lost in the wind.

She didn't know all the Scriptures. She didn't always know what to say.

But she knew how to stay.

And in the staying, others found their way. Just as she had. Just as Colocho once did.

The lamb that stayed had become a light of her own.

And the dawn, once again, began to dance.

From a Distance…

Jude stood at the ridge, his journal resting beside him, filled with his own prayers and God's words written in the margins of grace.

He observed the lambs gather again.

There was one in particular who caught his eye—the quiet one, the first to stay behind after the revival.

She moved with peace. She waited with purpose.

He whispered, almost without thinking, "Selah. That's your name."

It meant to pause and reflect. To rest. To stay.

He didn't need signs anymore. He simply lived in them.

The cross rested against his chest. The wind carried the name again.

Yahweh.

REFLECTIONS:

The SUNRISE Way

Let each morning rise not only with light, but with purpose and prayer. This path is simple. Quiet. Gentle. Like the Shepherd's call.

Colocho didn't discover a formula—he discovered a rhythm.

A way of being with God.

A way of living from peace, not just chasing it.

Each letter of SUNRISE reflects one of the seven relationship builders he discovered along the shore. These are meant to be read at dawn, in quiet moments, or whenever your heart forgets that you are being led.

You are not alone.

The Shepherd is calling.

Yahweh is calling.

God is calling.

And in the dawn, He still whispers your name.

S—Surrender to God, the Good Shepherd

> *Trust in the Lord with all your heart, and*
> *lean not on your own understanding; In all*
> *your ways acknowledge Him, and He shall*
> *direct your paths.—Proverbs 3:5–6 (NKJV)*

True surrender begins not with weakness, but with willingness.

Like Colocho stepping into the waves, we find our greatest strength when we stop striving and start trusting. The Shepherd's current may be invisible, but it is sure.

Reflect: What are you still trying to carry that God is asking you to lay down?

U—Unhurried Time

In quietness and trust is your strength.
—Isaiah 30:15 (NASB)

Faith is not forged in frenzy. It is formed in stillness.

Colocho learned this lying in the sand beside the turtle—watching the dawn unfold one quiet moment at a time. We're not called to rush with God, but to walk with Him.

Reflect: Where are you hurrying through what God wants you to linger in?

N—No Distractions

> *Be still, and know that I am God.*
> *—Psalm 46:10 (NKJV)*

The world rattles like a warning snake.

Not all distractions are evil—but most are empty.

Colocho learned to move behind the dunes, where the noise couldn't follow, and the Shepherd's whisper could finally be heard.

Reflect: What is drawing your attention away from God more than toward Him?

R—Reflect on My Path

Search me, God, and know my heart…lead me in the way everlasting.—Psalm 139:23–24 (NIV)

Reflection is not regret. It is remembering with purpose.

Colocho faced his fears beside the wolf—not to relive pain, but to see how far he had come. Reflection lets us trace the Shepherd's footprints where we once saw only our own.

Reflect: What part of your past might reveal God's presence if you looked again?

I—Intentional Quietness

*The Lord will fight for you; you need only
to be still.—Exodus 14:14 (NIV)*

The heron, wounded but wise, taught Colocho that quietness isn't emptiness—it's invitation. It is in the stillness that Yahweh's voice becomes most clear. And sometimes, the most powerful prayer is simply listening.

Reflect: When and where can you step away to hear God without interruption?

S—Scripture of the Day

> *Your word is a lamp to my feet and a light to my path.*—Psalm 119:105 (NASB)

When Colocho saw the verse written in the clouds, it lit more than the sky—it lit his path.

Scripture isn't just information. It's illumination. It doesn't only answer questions—it teaches us how to walk.

Reflect: What verse is lighting your way right now? Where do you need God's Word to guide you?

E—Enjoying Time with God

> *In Your presence is fullness of joy.*
> *—Psalm 16:11 (NASB)*

Colocho danced. Not because it was expected, but because it was the natural overflow of time spent with God. Joy is not a reward—it is a response.

You don't have to earn it. You just have to enter it.

Reflect: When was the last time you enjoyed God—fully, freely, without agenda?

Final Thought

The dawn is more than a moment.

It's a movement.

A daily call to pause, breathe, and begin again.

May each day you rise carry the rhythm of surrender, stillness, and joy.

May each morning lead you home.

Yahweh is calling.

And He still knows your name.

ACKNOWLEDGMENTS

First and always, I thank God—the Shepherd—for whispering this story into being and walking with me through every sunrise, every pause, and every page. This book is Yours.

To my wife, Leslie—your quiet strength and support made space for this book to grow. For over thirty years you've shared the journey, and in these last seasons you encouraged me when sunrise and beach time became part of our rhythm. You've been present in every page, seen and unseen.

To my daughter, Caitlin—thank you for inspiring me to keep creating, for your thoughtful feedback, and for reminding me through the years why stories matter. And to my parents, Martha and Jerry Koch—thank you for planting seeds of wisdom, love, and belief in me from the start. Together, you have been a steady source of encouragement and grounding, shaping both the man and the story.

To Joel—one of the shepherds God placed in my life—thank you for leading with humility and truth. And to the sheep who walked with me under that guidance—Patrick and Justin—your stories, friendship, and faith live in these pages as well.

To the Worship at Sunrise community—thank you for showing up every morning, and for reminding me that sunrise is never just for one soul. You've taught me that we are all still being led.

And to those who helped bring Colocho's story into its final shape—Kristen Stieffel, whose careful editing sharpened the words; Ines Monnet, whose steady hand shaped the pages; and Brad Bylund, whose brush brought Colocho to life on the cover, capturing the spirit of the story in color and light—I am deeply grateful. Together, your gifts formed a circle of clarity, beauty, and imagination around this book.

My prayer is that this book reaches those who need it—quietly, gently, just as it found me. May it always lead hearts back to the Shepherd.

ABOUT THE AUTHOR

Curtis Koch is a storyteller and sunrise walker whose early morning steps along the beaches of Galveston, Texas, first stirred quiet reflections. What began as simple weekend pauses soon became a life-giving rhythm of prayer, scripture, and reflection—what he now calls the SUNRISE way of life.

Out of that rhythm grew *Worship at Sunrise*, a small but growing community of people learning to listen for God at dawn. Still in its early steps, it is less an institution than a shared practice—one that may grow into a ministry of encouragement and quiet reflection.

Colocho: A Sheep on the Beach tells the SUNRISE story, the first in a series of fables born from these walks. Each story springs from real encounters by the shore, reimagined through the lens of faith, surrender, and transformation.

Curtis writes to help others slow down, ask honest questions, and draw closer to the God who calls gently through the waves—and whispers through every sunrise.

www.ingramcontent.com/pod-product-compliance
Lightning Source LLC
Chambersburg PA
CBHW042032120726
47911CB00026B/692